# I dream of trains

by Angela Johnson

*illustrated by* Loren Long

Simon & Schuster Books for Young Readers
New York    London    Toronto    Sydney    Singapore

**Papa tells me** Casey Jones started dreaming about trains
when he was littler than me.
I think of that—of big ol' Casey being littler than me—
and smile.

I dream of trains too.

As the Mississippi morning gets hotter

and red dirt sticks to my feet, making them heavy.

While the pickin' hurts my back.

I look over the long white rows and listen for Casey's whistle. . . .

Dreaming of trains.

When the cotton's all gone,

I'm still dreaming.

I walk along the tracks, and soon it's just us.

Me, Casey Jones, and his fireman, Sim Webb—

We work together as the engine carries us past the delta and across the plains.

Over the mountains, past the desert, and to the ocean—far away from here.

Along the way we look at people, and places,
then Casey lets me drive the engine.

And somewhere along the plains,

Casey lifts me up toward the magic,

and I sound the whistle. . . .

Some sounds can remind you of times gone by,

and as I blow the whistle

I remember that I am walking along the Mississippi tracks

dreaming of this. . . .

Soon I'm back beside my tracks,

missing Casey and Sim

and the feel of the whistle

speaking to me.

Papa says it's the sound of leaving

that speaks to my soul,

on through the daytime

that lingers on through the night. . . .

"Casey Jones knows," Papa says.

"Casey Jones must know."

Short days, cold days,

turn back into long, warm planting days,

and we are where we were and who we are.


I still stare at the tracks and wait for Casey and his

engine to come flying past the fields

and dream me away.

But then, one rainy April night, just up 'round Vaughan,

they say the rain was pouring worse than anybody had seen in years.

But Casey Jones and Sim Webb took the 382 out into the night.

Casey was doing a favor, 'cause it wasn't really his run,

and he was making up time—flying—

and didn't see the train ahead. The full train, up ahead.

Papa says that before the wreck came,

Casey sounded his whistle through the rain.

He grabbed the brake and the whistle,

warning everybody he was coming.

Holding fast, he told Sim Webb to jump

into the dark night.

Papa says they found him

with the brake still in his hand. . . .

I ask Papa,

"Does that mean it's over?"

We stand beside the spot

where Casey's engine 382 finally came to rest

Papa says, "No, there'll be other trains and engines."

Then he talks to me about the big wide world—

and the oceans and cities

and mountains that I'll one day see.


When Papa squeezes my hand I know

I have another hero besides Casey.

I walk slowly home with him and

I think of Casey with his hand on the whistle

and his other hand on the brake.

Too soon the rows of white cotton

come back to us all.

And I bend and pick,

pick and bend

beside my family,

and listen for the whistle

that blows past us

but doesn't speak to our souls.

When it's cool again, I walk the woods
and think of big ol' Casey and the cry of his whistle
dreaming me away.
Dreaming me away . . .

One day, when I am older,

I will leave the cotton behind.

I'll miss my family and the woods—

all that made me smile. . . .


But when my time comes for leaving,

I will take a train and

remember as I roll away

what Papa said about Casey

and his soul-speaking whistles

and my place in the big wide world.

**To Alyssa and DJ—*A. J.***

**For Tracy, Crazy Love . . . always—*L. L.***

## A NOTE ON THIS BOOK

At the turn of the twentieth century, black sharecroppers up and down the Mississippi Delta toiled long hours in fields alongside the route of Illinois Central's *Cannonball,* which John Luther "Casey" Jones drove back and forth between Canton, Mississippi, and Memphis, Tennessee. To the many men, women, and children along his route, the sight of Casey's massive engine barreling north and the long, drawn-out call of his trademark whistle must have been a symbol of hope. Moreover, the fact that Irish Casey worked side by side with black Webb probably did much to fuel the imaginations of a people who still remembered the sting of slavery and longed for an opportunity to be seen as equals with their fellow Americans. So it is completely understandable that Casey's tragic death one stormy night late in April 1900 would have such a tremendous impact on a disenfranchised black community with far too few heroes. And while the event was soon forgotten by most, Casey's life and death became the stuff of songs and stories for the black rail workers who worked on the IC Line. It was one of those workers, Wallace Saunders, who authored the ballad that is still sung in countless versions to this day.

And it's interesting to note that Casey's death occurred at the beginning of a period when countless blacks abandoned the oppressive South in search of new opportunities in cities like New York and Chicago. Historians commonly refer to the period as the Great Migration. How many of those individuals first got the idea to flee North from watching Casey's majestic engine? One can only wonder.

Illustrator acknowledgments: With my very first reading of Angela Johnson's words, countless images flew into my head. Thank you to Angela for this visual and truly meaningful manuscript.

Publisher acknowledgments: Much appreciation to Norma Taylor, historian at the Casey Jones Home and Railroad Museum, for her valuable insight. For more information about Casey Jones, write to the Casey Jones Home and Railroad Museum, 56 Casey Jones Lane, Jackson, Tennessee 38305-2451.

SIMON & SCHUSTER BOOKS FOR YOUNG READERS • An imprint of Simon & Schuster Children's Publishing Division • 1230 Avenue of the Americas, New York, New York 10020 • Text copyright © 2003 by Angela Johnson • Illustrations copyright © 2003 by Loren Long • All rights reserved, including the right of reproduction in whole or in part in any form. • SIMON & SCHUSTER BOOKS FOR YOUNG READERS is a trademark of Simon & Schuster. Book design by Dan Potash • The text of this book is set in Wilke. • The illustrations are rendered in acrylics. • Manufactured in China • 10 9 8 7 6 Library of Congress Cataloging-in-Publication Data • Johnson, Angela. • Casey Jones / by Angela Johnson ; illustrated by Loren Long.—1st ed. p. cm. Summary: The son of a sharecropper dreams of leaving Mississippi on a train with the legendary engineer Casey Jones • ISBN 0-689-82609-5 (hc) [1. Jones, Casey, 1863–1900—Juvenile fiction. [1. Jones, Casey, 1863–1900—Fiction 2. Railroads—Fiction. 3. Cotton picking—Fiction. 4. Fathers and sons—Fiction. 5. Mississippi—Fiction.] I. Long, Loren, ill. II. Title. PZ7.J629 Cas 2000 [E]—dc21 98-052886